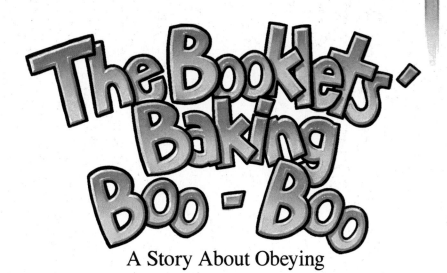

The Booklets' Baking Boo - Boo

A Story About Obeying

Featuring the Psalty family of characters
created by Ernie and Debby Rettino

Written by Ken Gire
Illustrated by John Dickenson,
Matt Mew, and Bob Payne

Published by Focus on the Family Publishing/Maranatha! for Kids

P. O. Box 500, Arcadia, CA 91006. Distributed by Word Books, Waco, Texas.

Library of Congress Catalog Card Number 87-81592
ISBN 084-9999-960

"Mom! Mom!" shouted Harmony as she came running into the kitchen with Melody and Rhythm right behind her. "I've got a first-rate idea! Can we bake a cake?"

"Yes, can we, Mom? Please?" echoed Melody.

"A chocolate one, okay?" chimed in Rhythm.

"No, not right now," said their mother Psaltina. "I need to go to the grocery store."

"Phooey, no cake," Rhythm grumbled, sticking out his lower lip.

"But tonight I'll bake you a big cake—chocolate, with lots of chocolate frosting," Psaltina promised, ruffling Rhythm's hair as she turned to leave.

The booklets watched through the window as Psaltina waved good-bye to their father Psalty, who was raking leaves in the front yard.

As she turned the corner, Rhythm spoke up: "I hate the word 'no.' It's the worst word in the whole wide world." He pressed his nose against the window and stared glumly outside.

"Hey, I've got an idea," Harmony exclaimed. "Let's surprise Mom and bake a cake while she's gone!"

"I don't know," replied Melody cautiously. "She said 'no.'"

"We could have it baked and frosted by the time she gets back," Harmony pointed out.

"Mmmm, chocolate cake right out of the oven! Sounds good to me," voted Rhythm.

And so they set out to bake the biggest, best, most beautimous cake ever!

Harmony grabbed the cookbook. Melody got the aprons. Rhythm found the spoon, bowl, and measuring cup.

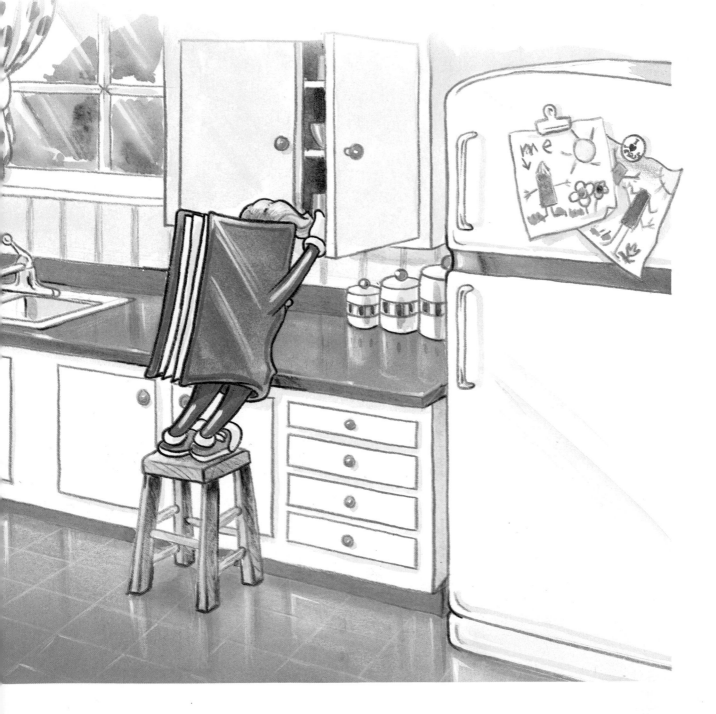

Harmony thumbed through the recipes until she came to a picture of the biggest, best, most beautimous cake in the entire cookbook.

"Oh, boy!" exclaimed Rhythm, spotting the cake. "I can almost taste it now. Hurry, let's get shaking and baking!"

"Let's see," Harmony pondered, studying the recipe, "we'll need flour and sugar and milk and eggs and butter and baking powder and—"

"Whoa, one at a time, Harmony," protested Melody, still searching the cupboards for the flour.

"Four cups of flour," said Harmony more slowly.

"We're all out of flour," responded Melody, peering inside the empty canister. "Can we use something else?"

"How about a flower from the backyard?" suggested Rhythm.

"No, that's a different kind of flower," Harmony said with a giggle.

"How about yeast?" asked Melody, rummaging around the cupboard. "Mom bakes with yeast a lot, doesn't she?"

"Sure she does, all the time," assured Harmony.

So they emptied out all the yeast packets until they had four cupsful.

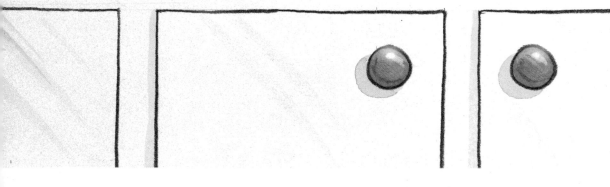

"What next?" Rhythm asked, impatient to get his mouth wrapped around a piece of this beautimous cake.

"Butter—half a cup," read Harmony.

"We don't have any butter," answered Melody, hunting through the refrigerator.

"Here's some peanut butter," volunteered Rhythm, his voice coming from deep inside a cupboard.

"Yes, peanut butter," his two sisters echoed. "That ought to work just as well."

"Now what?" Rhythm asked after emptying all the peanut butter into the bowl.

"One cup of sugar," said Harmony.

"Just one?" Rhythm asked with disappointment. "I like my cake really sweet."

"Me, too," agreed Melody.

So they put in a whole bag of sugar, along with a box of chocolates, a bunch of candy bars, and all sorts of other goodies they thought would make a great cake—like bubble gum and gummi bears and granola bars.

They took turns stirring the batter in the big bowl. It was much harder work than they had expected—and messier. Soon their aprons were spattered with batter. The mixture covered their hands. And some was even smudged on their faces. They all marched off to wash up in the bathroom sink.

But when they got back, the yeast in the cake had caused the mix to grow and GROW and *GROW*!

In fact, it had grown into a big blob that reached from the floor to the ceiling, and covered the entire kitchen. It was hu-u-uge.

"Oh, no!" shouted Rhythm. Harmony and Melody just stood there with their mouths open in surprise and horror.

"Hurry!" Rhythm exclaimed. "Let's *do* something quick! Mom will be home any minute!"

Suddenly the door opened, and Psaltina walked in, carrying a big bag of groceries. But the sack dropped with a thud when she saw the blob covering her whole kitchen.

"We're sorry, Mom," the booklets apologized, looking at her sadly. "We tried to bake the cake by ourselves."

"That's a cake?" Psaltina asked in surprise. Then she said sternly: "I thought I told you, 'No, you can't bake a cake'?"

The booklets lowered their heads and nodded slowly, hoping their mother would see how sorry they were.

"Mom, can you ever forgive us?" Rhythm asked.

"Of course I forgive you," she told them and gave each of them a hug, despite the batter spattered on their aprons. "But there's still the kitchen to clean up," she pointed out.

She thought for a minute and studied the immense blob. Then she walked to the doorway and called out: "Psalty, come quick! And bring your rake and trash bags!"

Psalty rushed in but stopped short when he saw the blob that had taken over the kitchen. ''What's that?'' he asked in surprise.

''It was going to be the biggest, best, most beautimous cake ever,'' Harmony said, remembering the cake pictured in the cookbook.

The whole family started to work. Psalty raked lumps of batter into the bags. Psaltina used a broom. The booklets scooped up the goop with their hands.

Each clump landed in the trash with a sound like PALUMP. In all, the batter filled fifty-eight bags!

When the mess was cleaned up, they looked at each other and all burst out laughing at the same time. They had been so busy that they didn't notice how much of the batter had gotten into their hair, on their faces, and all over their book covers.

"Everybody outside," ordered Psalty, and they all washed up with the hose. The cold water made the booklets squeal "E-e-e-ek!" but it felt good to be clean again.

Then they went inside to help Psaltina put away the groceries that she had dropped.

"Flour," said Harmony, picking up the five-pound bag from the floor.

"And butter," added Rhythm.

"That's why we couldn't bake a cake," Psaltina pointed out. "We didn't have the right ingredients."

The booklets all felt bad as they realized why their mother had said "no."

"Don't put those in the cupboard," Psaltina said to the booklets as they started putting away the groceries.

"Why not?" asked Harmony.

"Because we'll need those ingredients to bake our cake."

All the booklets looked at each other and cheered: "Oh, boy! Oh, boy! A cake! We'll bake a cake! Yummy, yummy, yummy!"

Step by step, Psaltina went through the recipe with them, explaining what each ingredient was and what it did. She told them how important it was to follow all the directions in the recipe. If they disobeyed just one, it might ruin the whole cake.

When the cake came out of the oven, everyone gathered around it and sniffed the luscious chocolate smell as it filled the air.

''What are we waiting for?'' demanded Rhythm. ''Let's frost it and have a slice.''

''No, Rhythm. It has to cool first,'' Psaltina pointed out.

There was that word again—''no.'' But Rhythm obeyed his mom this time and waited.

When the cake cooled, they all took turns frosting it. And before you could say, ''biggest, best, most beautimous cake ever,'' it was all done.

The family sat around the table as Psaltina cut each one a big, yummy slice of cake. Psalty poured each one a tall glass of ice-cold milk.

They all dug into the cake with hardly a word spoken because it was so-o-o-o-o delicious!

You could only hear the sound of forks scraping plates until Rhythm spoke up: "You know, Mom, I've been thinking. Sometimes I forget you have reasons for not letting us do what we want."

"I know, Rhythm," Psaltina responded. "It's hard to remember, isn't it?"

"Yes, Mom, but I've been thinking something else, too," Rhythm added. "I've been thinking that maybe 'no' isn't such a bad word after all!"

Psaltina just smiled and ruffled Rhythm's hair.